THE FINAL STAND

Adapted by
Tennant Redbank

Illustrated by
Judie Clarke, Samantha Clarke, Caroline Egan

Designed by
Disney's Global Design Group

Random House 🏠 New York

Milo Thatch had never imagined that the expedition would turn out like this. He'd led that villain Commander Rourke right to Atlantis. Now Rourke had stolen the Crystal, the Atlanteans' life force, with Princess Kida crystallized inside it.

"In times of danger," said the king of Atlantis, "the Crystal will choose a host, one of royal blood, to protect itself and its people."

But who would protect Atlantis now that the Crystal had been taken away? Milo looked at the small crystal in his hand— the king's own crystal. Then Milo rose to his feet and strode out of the room.

Outside the palace, the rest of the expedition crew and the Atlanteans watched as Milo climbed onto a stone vehicle shaped like a fish. "I'm going after Rourke," said Milo. He inserted the king's crystal into the keyhole and put his hand on the control pad. In a flash, the fish rose off the ground.

Everyone rushed to other stone fish vehicles—Aktiraks, Ketaks, and Martags—and started them up. Even Milo's fellow crew members Audrey, Dr. Sweet, Mole, and Vinny joined in. The new Atlantean armada was on the move!

Ka-BOOm!

Inside a nearby volcano shaft, a cannon blew a hole in the top of the volcano. This was Rourke's escape route to the surface. He smiled at his lieutenant, Helga. "I love it when I win," he said.

Behind him, a trooper removed the top of the water tanker. Hidden inside was a hot-air balloon called the gyro-evac, which began to inflate automatically. The trooper attached chains to secure the transport pod containing Kida, the crystallized princess, to the gyro-evac. Then Rourke and Helga climbed aboard, and the gyro-evac began to rise.

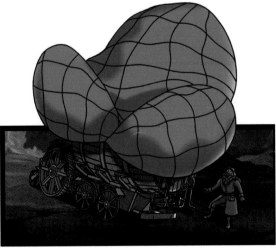

Milo and the armada emerged from an underground cave and spotted Helga and Rourke making their getaway. "There they are!" Milo shouted.

Rourke's troopers opened fire. The Atlanteans shot back with spears and bows and arrows. The battle raged.

Then Vinny accidentally leaned on a button on his Martag. Out shot a laser beam, taking out one of the troopers' trucks!

"Okay, now things are getting good!" Vinny shouted.

Audrey, Dr. Sweet, and Mole veered away from the battle. They couldn't let Rourke escape with Kida! They guided their Martag until it hovered under the princess pod. Then Audrey scrambled up and tried to saw through the chains. But they were too thick!

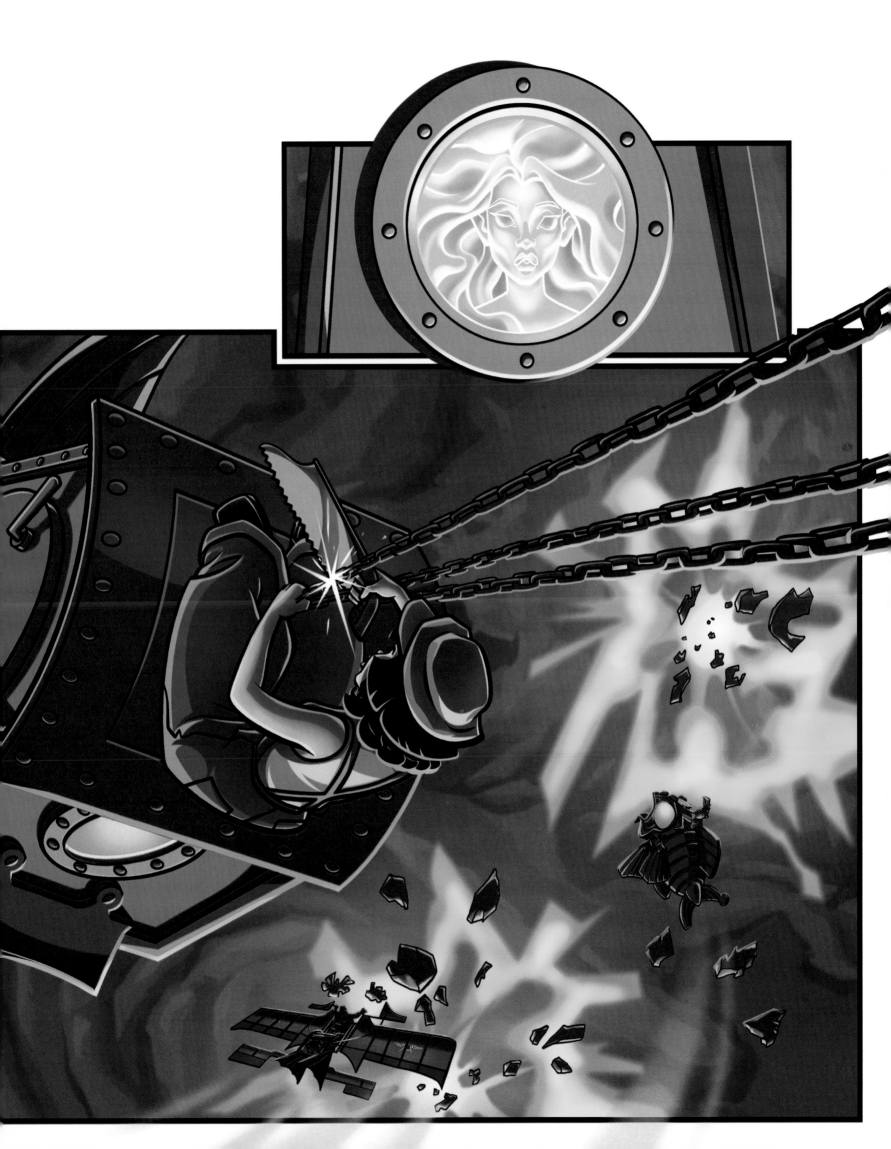

 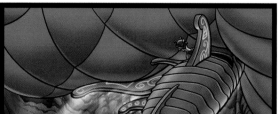 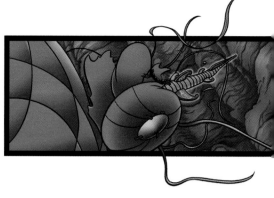

Meanwhile, Milo steered
his Aktirak straight at
the gyro-evac. When he
was within a few feet of
the balloon, he balanced
on his vehicle and leaped
through the air, barely
catching hold of the
netting that covered the
gyro-evac. At the same
moment, his Aktirak—now
without a driver—ripped
a hole in the balloon.

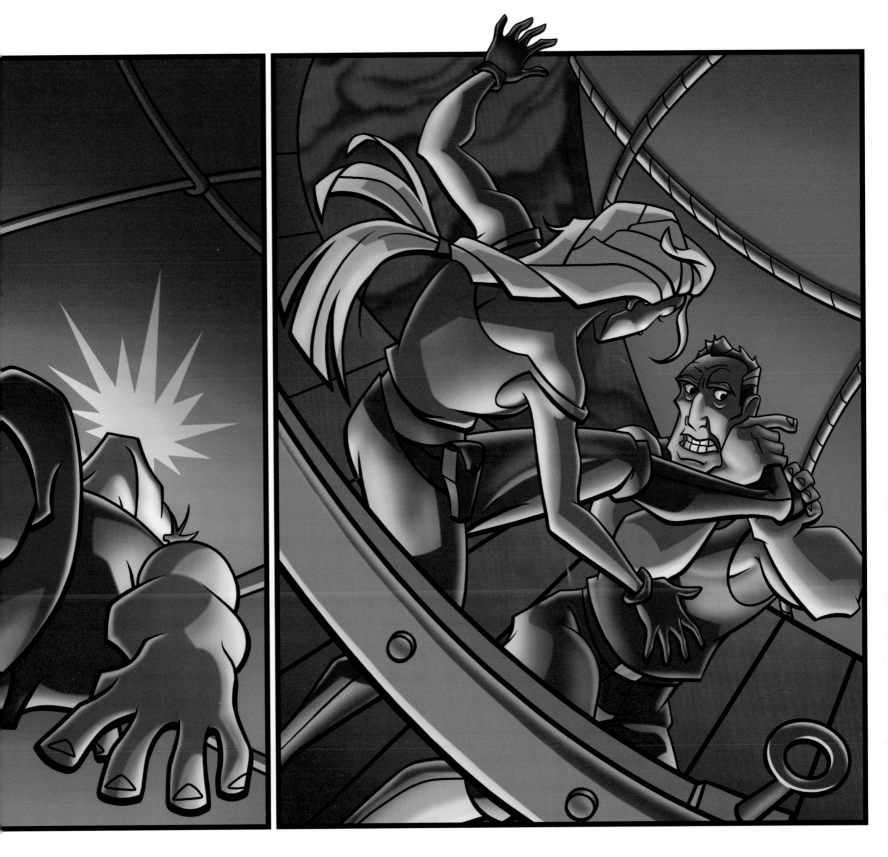

"We're losing altitude," Rourke said. He had to lighten
the load. Rourke eyed Helga. When her back was turned,
he pushed her over the side. Helga grabbed the railing
and swung herself back up, but Rourke managed to toss
her out of the gyro-evac again—this time for good.

Rourke shrugged. "Nothing personal."

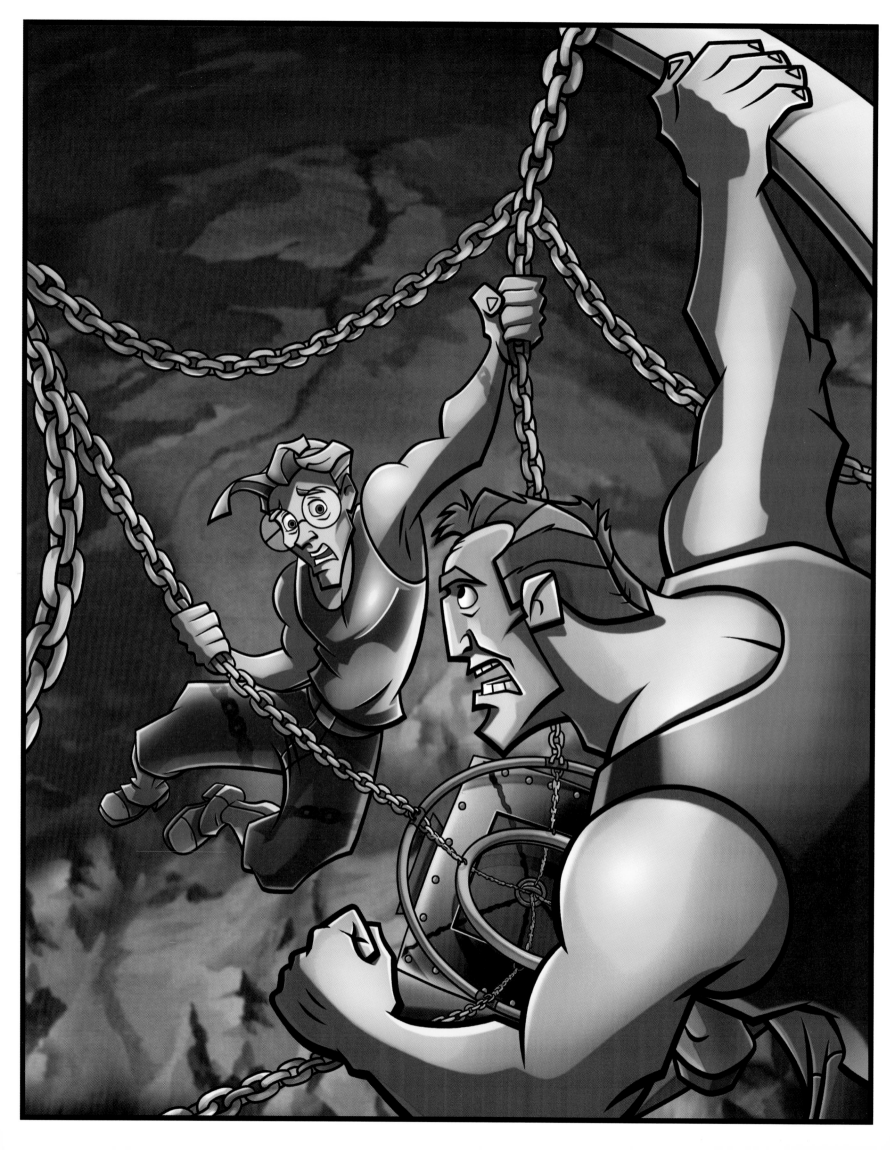

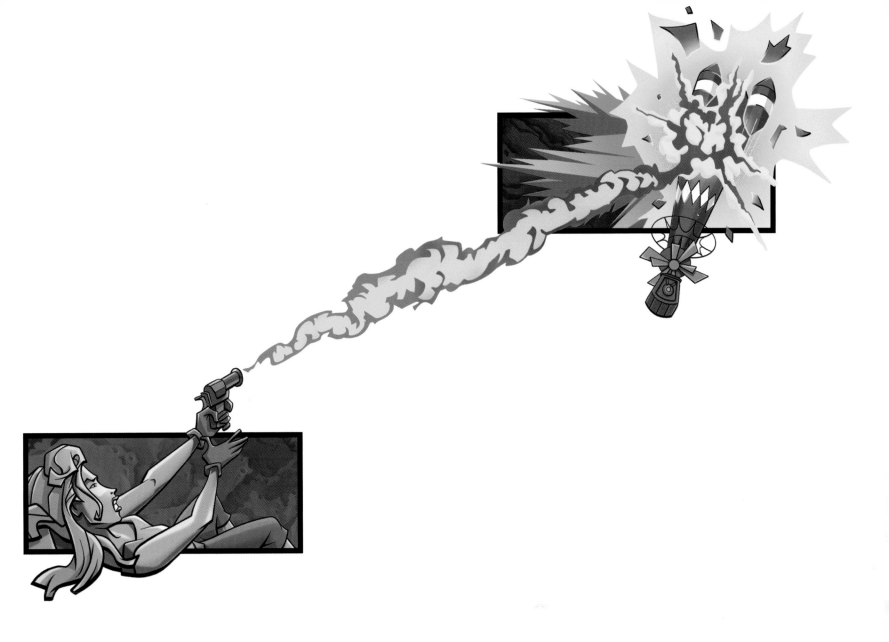

Seconds later, Milo swung down from above, knocking Rourke off his feet. But Rourke recovered quickly. "You're a bigger pain in the neck than I would have ever thought possible," he said. He kicked Milo through the side railing. Luckily, Milo caught hold of the chains that held the princess pod.

Suddenly, a flare tore into the balloon, setting it on fire. On the ground, Helga, barely alive, lowered her flare gun. "Nothing personal," she echoed.

Rourke grabbed an ax from the emergency casing in the gyro-evac and climbed down after Milo.

Ah-aHhh!

Rourke swung the ax. Milo ducked. The ax struck the pod, shattering the window. Desperately, Milo plucked out a shard of glass that glowed with Crystal energy. Then, as Rourke grabbed Milo by the throat, Milo cut Rourke's arm with the shard.

Rourke's grip loosened. A blue light traveled up his arm, turning his flesh to crystal. The Crystal recognized Rourke's evil, turning him an angry red, then black. Then he hardened into a crystallized statue.

When Rourke got in the way of the gyro-evac's massive spinning blades, his crystalline body shattered.

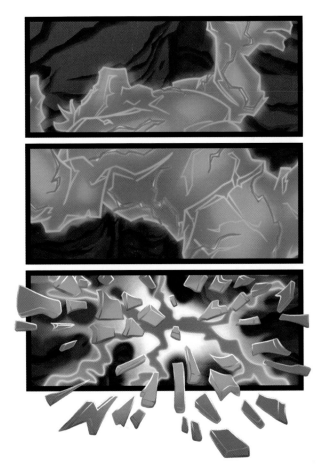

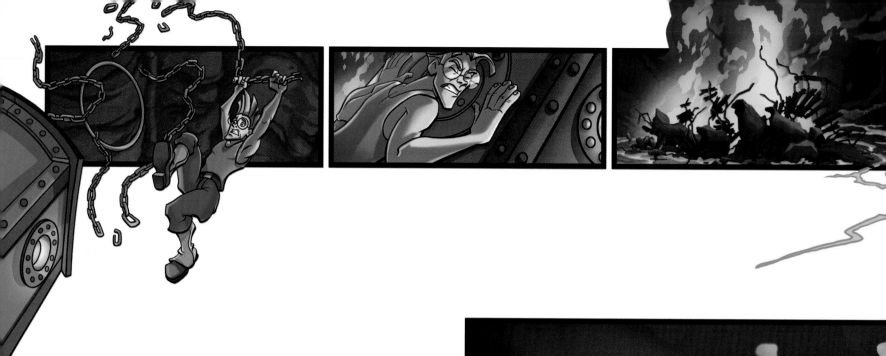

Moments later, Milo heard a snap. The chains had broken and the princess pod fell to the ground. Milo jumped down after it! With all his strength, he pushed the pod out of harm's way, only seconds before the gyro-evac crashed to the ground and exploded.

The force of the explosion reached underground, setting off a chain reaction.

"The volcano . . . she awakes!" Mole shouted.

They had to get out of there! Quickly, Milo wrapped
a chain around the pod while Audrey and Vinny attached
the other end to the back of their Martag. "Go!" Milo
shouted to his friends. He held the chain in place as
the stone fish lifted off. They outran the fiery lava
and raced back to Atlantis.

In the center plaza of Atlantis, Audrey gently lowered the princess pod to the ground. Milo pried it open with a spear. Suddenly, the walls of the pod flew off. Kida hovered in the air, glowing with the life energy of the city.

Beneath the plaza, the King Stones—statues of past Atlantean kings—also began to glow, brought to life by the crystallized Kida's return. They pushed up through the ground and rose to surround Kida in midair. They whirled around her, faster and faster. She glowed brighter than a star and beams of light shot from her body.

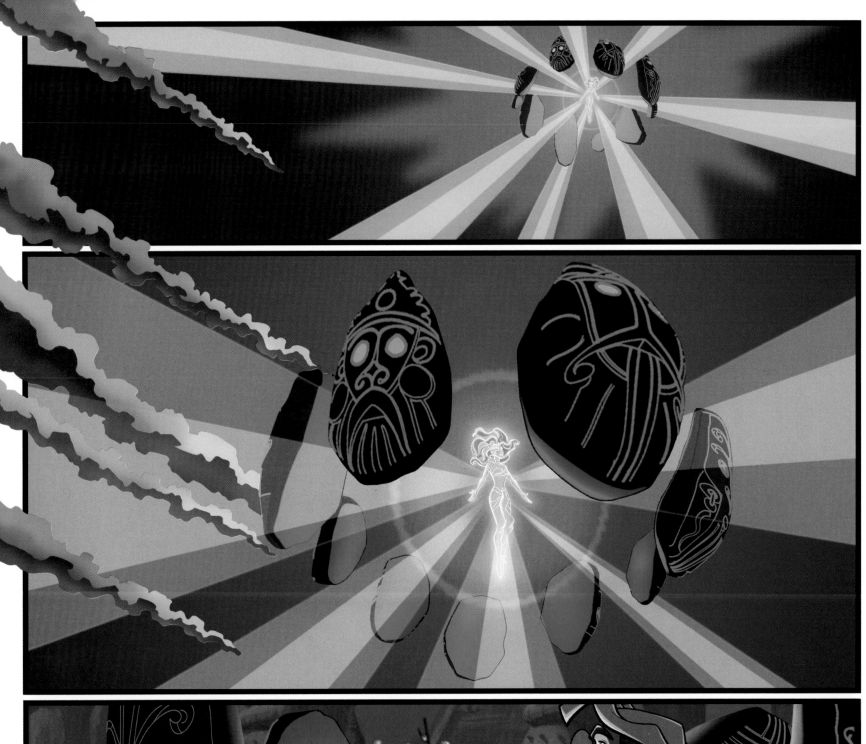

One by one, the beams of light fell on the Stone Giants that lay throughout the city. The guardians rose like people waking from a long sleep. They formed a ring around Atlantis.

Then, as they clapped their stone hands, a protective dome of energy covered the city—just as the huge wave of lava broke.

The lava flowed harmlessly up the sides of the dome. Milo had done it! He had saved Kida and Atlantis!

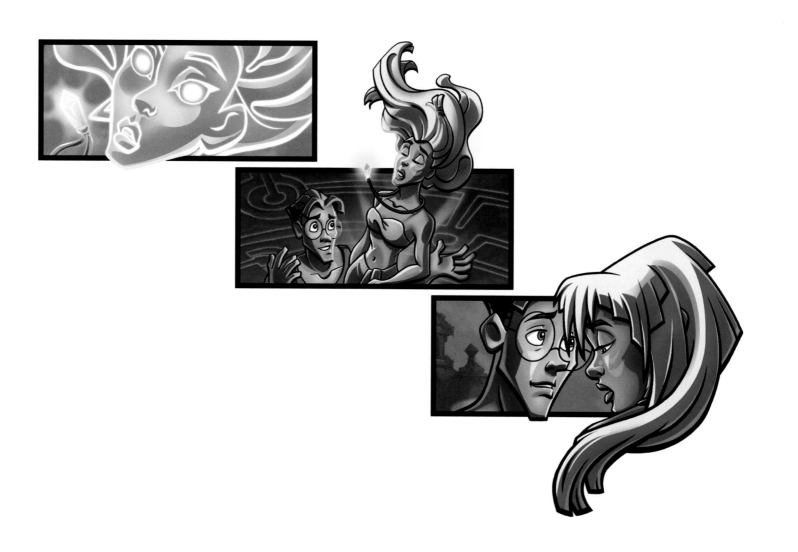

The lava cooled, cracked, and fell away. Above the plaza, Kida's glow faded. Her crystalline form dissolved and she turned back into the Atlantean princess Milo knew. Her destiny fulfilled, Kida floated gently down into Milo's arms.

"Milo," she said weakly. Milo just smiled and held her tightly as the steam cleared to reveal a beautiful new Atlantis. The Atlantis of the past . . . and of their future together.

All rights reserved under International and Pan-American Copyright Conventions. Published in the United States by
Random House, Inc., New York, and simultaneously in Canada by Random House of Canada Limited, Toronto,
in conjunction with Disney Enterprises, Inc. RANDOM HOUSE and colophon are registered trademarks of Random House, Inc.
Library of Congress Card Catalog Number: 00-108353
ISBN: 0-7364-1083-X

Printed in the United States of America
May 2001
10 9 8 7 6 5 4 3 2 1

www.randomhouse.com/kids/disney
www.disneybooks.com